Circles of R⬤und

Written by Signe Sturup

Illustrated by Winnie Ma

Simply Read Books

Once upon a time, in a town called Round, there lived Circles who were kind and fun-loving.

The Circles of Round lived in circular houses.
They had circular ways and lived circular days.
They rolled to school. They rolled to work.

And life rolled merrily along.

Despite the odd bump in the road,
life in Round was peaceful.

BUT...

He's obtuse!

One day a stranger came to Round.
Gossip circulated.

How profound!

No Circle at all…

the newcomer was a Triangle!

Curious, the Circles
crowded 'round the Triangle.

"Circles, are you tired of just rolling through life? Are you in poor shape? Perhaps you need a better one! I introduce to you the Corner Transformer."

"It's terrific to be Triangular and it's hip to be Square! For only a few coins you can give it a spin! It's sure to give you a new angle on life. Just look what you and your town could become!"

"OOOooOOooooooo!"

The Triangle was very persuasive.
He took out an ad in the Circular Times.
He marched through town with slogans
and signs. Eventually, the Circles decided
they just had to try it!

With their coins going clinkety-clink,
the Circles rolled up to try the Corner Transformer.

Some became Triangles. Some became Squares.
And some…well…some got a bit carried away.

But their new angles on life created some strife. Although they looked edgy, the new shapes of Round stumbled upon a whirlwind of bad points.

Their corners made tears

in their beds and their chairs.

They ripped up their houses

and tore through the streets.

The smallest of the Squares was extremely
unhappy. He could no longer cycle to school
or play ball in the park. Loop-the-Loop was
out and Ring-Around-the-Rosy became a
distant memory. Facing the rest of his life
as a Square was unbearable.

So he thought of how to
become round again.

He thought

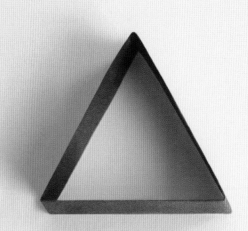

and he thought

and he thought

and he thought

and he thought *SO* hard that…

The sweaty Squares and tired Triangles
ogled the little Circlet as he rolled by
with ease. They got the point at once.
Round was the way to be.

"Come! You can roll again too!
Concentrate hard!" the Circlet said.

"Just think out your kinks!"

Now that everybody was rounded up,
they rolled to the Triangle.

"Squares may be hip and Triangles
trendy but Circles have class.
We don't need to be bendy!"

The Triangle realized this market could never be cornered. He packed up his goods and vanished that day.

The Circles had learned from their mistake.
They thought things through, and in turn, they grew.

Over the years, they grew and they grew...

into wise old Spheres.

Published in 2013 by Simply Read Books Inc. www.simplyreadbooks.com
Text © 2013 Signe Sturup
Illustrations © 2013 Winnie Ma

Sturup, Signe   Circles of round / by Signe Sturup ; and illustrated by Winnie Ma.
ISBN 978-1-927018-18-7
          I. Ma, Winnie II. Title.
PS8637.T88C57 2012   jC813'.6   C2012-903680-3

We gratefully acknowledge for their financial support of our publishing program the
Canada Council for the Arts, the BC Arts Council, and the Government of Canada
through the Canada Book Fund (CBF).

Manufactured in Malaysia.

Book design by Winnie Ma

The illustrations in this book were created using cut paper.

10 9 8 7 6 5 4 3 2 1